THE CHILD
THAT WOULD BE MISSED

ERIC SOWERS

Foyer Publishing

Richlands, North Carolina

Foyer Publishing

407 Jessica Court

Richlands, North Carolina

First Foyer Publishing Edition November 2021

For information about discounts on bulk purchases, please contact Foyer Publishing at (910) 430-9990 or email at pro@foyerpub.com

Foyer Publishing aids aspiring authors to share their stories at live events. To schedule your next event, email us at pro@foyerpub.com

Cover by Stephen Rocktaschel

Paperback ISBN 979-8-9851279-0-4

eBook ISBN 979-8-9851279-1-1

May we choose silence when we are too eager to speak

speak as though we are who we endeavor to be.

Dedication Page

Special thanks to Ionica (pronounced u-knee-ka) who constantly encouraged me through the completion of this book. Though we have never met in person, you've touched me in all the ways that truly matter.

And humble gratitude to my hero Mollie, who through being her best self, saved my life and showed me a sense of peace worth striving for.

Those closest to us are either the bars in our jail cell or the rungs in our ladder.

Table of Contents

Chapter 1: Romeo and Juliet Company 1

Key to Happiness 2

Living the Dream.. 3

Afterword 4

Messy Bed.. 5

New Me... 6

Mistletoe... 7

Adrift.. 8

Fairer Day.. 9

Where Love Is Found... 10

Bashful 12

Stratified Affection 13

Real As It Gets.. 15

Chapter 2: The Will to Fight 17

Clean... 18

Semper Why.. 19

Mr. Sandman 20

Walking On Fate... 21

Return Flight 22

Away for the Day 23

Stillness.. 24

A Platter.. 25

The Right Attitude 26

Where Is the Heart? 28

Blanch 29

Sit 31

Wonderful Lights 32

Cherish 33

The Bear and I 34

Kabul Sunset 36

Chapter 3: Rest and Relaxation **37**

Our Poem 38

Life and Liberty 40

Personal Ad 41

Kitchen Chorus 42

Comings and Goings 43

Through the Ups and Downs 45

Chapter 4: Sight Alignment and Sight Picture **47**

Global Climate Crisis 48

I Am the American Flag 49

Knowing Your Right......From Left 51

No Quarter 53

Melancholy 54

Silent Bee 55

Sky of Wonder 56

Wish Me Well 57

Can't Be 58

This Is It! 59

What Are You Looking At? 60

How Do I Reel In That Fish? 61

You Can't Fix Stupid 62

Heel of Achilles 63

Close Enough 64

A Drop of Water 65

Without Compare 66

Credits **67**

The Author **68**

CHAPTER 1

Romeo and Juliet Company

Key to Happiness

The sun and moon dance in the sky

As electrons and nuclei dance in your eye.

That eye then turns your world upside down,

Just like when yours is, you tear and frown.

In the blink of an eye, your brain shifts your view.

No longer fake, a smile has landed on your face,

Inviting everyone to the joy you now taste.

Love is why we all dance.

The ocean waves at the moon.

The owl never asks why.

The whale sings its tune

To an ear across the ocean

As two hearts skip a beat.

A chick falls from the nest.

A cat lands on her feet.

The world will turn as my tires burn.

Existence again continues to breathe.

Living the Dream

Dreaming of tomorrow,

Then missing yesterday

While missing so many sweet moments in front of me today.

A trickle, then barrage of plump, cold rain drops

On a summer afternoon,

Gliding down my cheeks as joyful tears,

Hailing from clouds on high,

Such sweet tasting water slides between my lips,

Rolling along my chin and drips,

Plunging to the planks below my feet.

I become a waterfall in this heavy downpour.

How rich I am in this moment,

Wealthy in breath in this sea of tranquility.

Afterword

I've been broken down to nothing

Without income, dollars, or sense,

Homeless in a far-off place,

Hopeless, sleeping alone, on a bus to nowhere.

Here approached a tattered man, living outside reality.

Sleeping more would have been so sweet, yet this treasure had been discarded

Just like me.

After walking many miles and hearing his folly-filled tales,

We continued on different trails.

Then I recalled a path where I had reached,

Ears were deaf, eyes wandered, and none would take my hand.

So, I reached for any numbing ally that would not judge or comprehend.

Tonight, under street light, in this land far from the place of my birth,

I'm without a friend at this dead end and of very little worth.

Yet soon, I would find my hand grasped,

As brazen heroes towed me back to my berth.

Docks repaired my rudder,

Gifting me a beating heart and a gold mind.

Now I reach out my hand to see you through,

To clench and not let go,

For if gravity won't do its job, I'll pull the earth to you.

Messy Bed

Nothing, is that? No—

The soft top of the naked mattress,

I need to put the sheets on the bed.

Absent light's shadows lays heavy upon me.

I've no inkling to see or be seen.

I have too much clutter on my bed,

So much to take time from me,

Moments moving them here and there,

Occupying my focus,

Moving me to need more.

I needed to sit here and love,

Love that being that I am,

Ginger tea on my tongue,

Gingerly flowing between my tastebuds,

Marvelous.

New Me

Tomorrow would be a new day

If there were anything new under the sun.

Yet new to me will come to be

Once today's child has begun.

I'll uncover that place inside of me,

Hidden under callused skin,

And get in touch with so much

Of the suffering that I've been in.

I'll brush my teeth and style my hair,

Lotion my skin and massage with care,

Shout, "I'm excited to be alive!"

Have no worries of negative flurries,

Accumulating sorrows up to my ears.

Perhaps I'll catch smiles and release some tears,

Being okay about not being okay.

What's new for me that I hope will be

Is me.

Mistletoe

Holding it over me,

Asking me to give you a kiss,

The ransom lest you blow me away,

Go ahead and blow me today.

You shot me in the back

And drug me back in the door,

Started my heart again,

For you wanted more.

I've given it all, now your tongue wants another taste.

Adrift

Drowning in the light,

Gasping for air in the dark,

Grasping for an anchor

To drag me down

In the calm, killing sea.

You are the salt in my water.

Drinking you drains me,

Yet I drink more,

Thirsting for rest.

Land is not far off,

Yet I drift

As kelp in the sea breeze.

Parched lips kissed by the sun,

My tongue twirls around you,

Swallowing, I choke.

Still, I breathe

Until still.

Fairer Day

Shame is something that needs to be let go.

Depression dines on regrets and grudges:

Lost loves, missed opportunities, and anxiety of what could be.

Be here now,

One more moment not feeding those phantoms

Nor the urge to be that fulfillment to someone else,

That lust, crutch, smile,

An amusement or abusement.

When you are no longer the caged bird that sings,

In that moment, you find your voice.

Where Love Is Found

So what the fuck, soul?

Like the sol that shines so bright?

Is your fire that burns so hot with anger

Worth burning all within your sight?

Will the spirits that mind drinks

To silence your raging wails

Get washed away by happy tears

When the reign of joy prevails?

J-O-Y, three letters work together

To show us how you feel

When calm and place

And warm embrace spell happiness for real.

A place to lay your head,

A smooth rock would be so nice,

When joy is a tent,

Warm fire,

And skin pressed firm yet gently.

Two speak through their bodies,

Comforted in each other's private space.

Warm firelight dancing in the night

On the beauty of your lover's face.

Yet this was never real!

Though this warm moment I now feel,

Not as memory or a dream

But enveloped in euphoria so surreal.

For in this perfect moment, if someone came to kill,

Having had this blissful time together

Means transcending from still to still,

Still in satisfaction without a place to run.

To still, laying in the dirt, just like everyone.

So, soul within me, speak! Here in this early hour.

Convey the thoughts mind needs to ponder

To find joy before I shower.

And when I shower, wash away

Stagnant thoughts of yesterday.

Then dry my face of water, and let happy tears flow.

For that elusive joy will be mine,

For mind and soul to know.

In this body, they will roll and embrace all the day,

Deep into the night.

They will make pure love that I can give

To everyone in sight.

So, my pyre will burn and blaze

But not those who draw close.

Firelight will warm their face

While we embrace

Joy for eternity.

Bashful

Love's rhapsodical arsenal crushes and permeates,

Piercing my armor, freeing cocooned butterflies.

Their fluttering wingtips strum my heartstrings.

Sounding the battle cry for the conquest of my essence.

Your aroma and caress are chemical and biological warfare,

Yet the love you give is your nuclear option,

And I will retaliate in kind.

Nothing will burn hotter than our passion,

As what was once invaluable turns to ash,

And our love is all that remains.

Stratified Affection

You are my anchor,

Heavy in compassion.

Therefore, you plunge very deep.

You smash through sunken ships

And scatter the bones of lost skeletons,

For the past is as gone as the next moment

Yet the hope of changing this eternal being in this moment

Is the kiss you give.

That kiss is like how each color of the rainbow kisses another,

And without each of those kisses, no rainbows could be.

How the sun kisses my skin in the moonlight,

Though I see no sun, and it is so far off, it's smile still shines on me,

And as the wind on a calm day gently tickles my lips

With the air that has been shoved out of the way

By colliding lips of all the generations,

Eager to touch and speak love,

Silently telling each other that the horrors of life are not powerful enough to stop us.

And as my passion sails on the solar winds to the edges of existence,

May every instance of energy know the high of being loved when love seems foreign,

When love is a phenomenon.

Let the unexplainable become all knowledge, all emotion, and all light.

I accept that I am loved by you,

Not knowing if you love me

But believing that your compassion and actions are of love.

I embrace it because I have so often rejected love shown to me,

Not feeling worthy to be connected to the cosmic river of life.

Floating with you toward the edge,

There is a massive waterfall.

We are at peace in emotion right now.

Yet slowly drifting toward the great descent,

Maybe we will never fall,

Maybe all the water that came before us fell,

Maybe we will be the ones who sail into the clouds

And rain down on a crying little child

And wash away their tears.

Real As It Gets

Your smile beats a cold beer after a fourteen-hour day in the sun.

Your smooth voice intoxicatingly flows into my ears,

Drowning my worries in delicious bliss.

Feeling your love, every blood cell in my body forms the shape of a heart.

CHAPTER 2

The Will to Fight

Clean

On an island in a swamp,
As I grew into a Marine,
I was taught to always stand tall
And to keep my honor clean.
Our squad bay was spotless all the day,
As we pushed dirty water out the door.
We scuzzed the deck, killing every speck
For our country and our corps.
Our drill instructors were crisp and sharp
With starched shirts and angelic voices.
They were our conscience in the darkness
In times of challenging
Lest we make immoral choices.
In war, we cleaned up each other
After being blasted across the land:
A hand, a foot covered in soot,
An honor so heavy some still can't stand.
Stand the memories of those we've lost,
Who are buried deep within our souls,
And family lost in lives we tossed
While digging our new foxholes.

Eric Sowers

Semper Why

One young lady recently asked of me

About a major event in my history,

How someone who thought of others, so kind and caring,

Chose a vocation that called for such violence and daring.

Silence the violins for all my woes.

Casualties mount in more than lives:

Thunder of explosions or fleeing spouses slamming doors,

Liquor on my tongue or in the dirt as it pours.

Yet all these are an afterthought

Of a career that took so much.

Marines have determination and unwavering courage,

Unstoppable in action, of which I've come to know to be true.

College did not entice me, for I knew what I wanted to do.

A veteran business owner offered me a career

If I chose not to join the Marines.

Medics in Vietnam saw the bloodiest scenes.

No, nothing then could change my mind.

To answer her question the truth is this,

I made the best decision at the time with the information available.

No one can do better than that.

Mr. Sandman

Somewhere in the sand,

Beyond that hill in a distant land,

Lay circles of sharp wire

That kept out young boys and girls.

As the wire came unfurled,

My rifle wanted to scream.

A girl and her younger brother played as if in a dream

Under a single tree on the hilltop,

Under the blue clear sky.

Clad in armor, my finger eager,

To pull and pull.

Tugging the noose around my inner child,

Barbed wire still rests around my heart,

Keeping my soul and life's precious treasures apart.

Walking On Fate

Some of the greatest warriors walking this earth have no legs.

Still, they run for their comrades who ran toward their fate.

Millions have lost those they cherish most while at their post,

And spouses have found that their partners have never really returned.

Some of the greatest warriors are still at war.

An infant cries as her father bombards her with words of rage.

A nine-year-old holds her tears as she learns that her mother's plane crashed.

An uncle wrestles with PTSD as his nephew pulls a trigger in his barracks room.

Whether we struggle to remember or drink to forget,

There is much fighting for these warriors yet.

Return Flight

As the turbulence shuddering this plane,

The past two weeks have been relentless.

My mother awaits death daily.

My marriage escapes death barely.

My soul tempts death within my thoughts.

I try to bury these monsters.

Now they breathe down my neck to remind me,

Unresolved grief always emerges.

Away for the Day

My mother was relieved the chemo was finished.

The cancer had spread through her whole body.

Giving her a hug,

I spoke my last words to her,

Bye, love you.

My mom wasn't gone. I was leaving.

Her eyes remained on her only child

As he marched toward the war.

Turning, her baby's hazel eyes met hers

For one last embrace,

Then departed her life forever.

I soared high over the Atlantic,

Back to Afghanistan,

Back to my Marines.

Young men and women,

Who were missing children being born,

Finding out the person they loved was leaving them

Or simply couldn't sit down to taste their Mama's cookin'.

Touching down at a crossroads,

Far from Lady Liberty's gaze,

Yet beyond the range of enemy mortars,

The bomb dropped on me.

Her pain was over.

Stillness

I didn't lose anything in the war.

I brought more back with me.

I lost people in the war.

I brought them back with me.

I didn't lose the war.

I'm still fighting the war.

I'm not sure if I'm winning.

I'm not sure why I'm fighting.

Why do I push those I love away

As if I just stepped on a landmine?

So they don't have to feel the burn

I feel all day.

A Platter

My fist slams, and hot marinara sauce splatters.

Across the table, wide-eyed diners hush,

No laughter or tears.

Inside I'm covered in frustration,

I continue to kill myself a little more

With each bite of obstinance.

I swallow.

It descends into the black hole devouring the light of my soul,

An unfillable abyss that I can only stomach since I placed it there.

With every concession to do that which I knew I should have refused,

Every failure that I allow myself to feel as if my pride is deflowered for the first time,

Lost in the paradox of my unattainable expectations and detested condition,

Yet forth I march, searching for that moment I matter,

To the one who ultimately matters in my life.

The Right Attitude

Fuck it all.

Fuck the tall,

Fuck the pretty,

And fuck the small.

Fuck the ugly,

Fuck the mad,

Fuck me, too,

And yes, fuck you.

Fuck the laughing,

Fuck sweet people with tears,

Fuck puppies so cute with their floppy ears,

May couples fucking be fucked in more ways than one,

Fuck the rising day, and fuck the setting sun.

Fuck night, fuck this moment, and fuck the calm breeze.

Fuck people who hurt you, fuck those you hurt,

Fuck the hateful, and fuck different people.

If I forgot anyone,

Let them be fucked abundantly and overrunning.

Eric Sowers

Replace fuck with love, and it will un-fuck you.

Love it all:

Love the tall,

Love the pretty,

And love the small.

Love the ugly,

Love the mad,

Love me, too,

And yes, love you.

Love the laughing,

Love sweet people with tears,

Love puppies so cute with their floppy ears,

May couples loving be loved in more ways than one,

Love the rising day, and love the setting sun.

Love night, love this moment, and love the calm breeze.

Love people who hurt you, love those you hurt,

Love the hateful, and love different people.

If I forgot anyone,

Let them be loved abundantly and overrunning.

Where Is the Heart?

We're trying to make it home,

A casa tucked away in our dreams.

Log cabin walls hug the warm love within

As sunshine glimmers off a drop diving from the kitchen faucet.

If stepping inside, the love is not there,

Walls of chipped paint depict the despair,

The dripping drop plops without the sun's glare

Followed by more tears of this homely nightmare.

We made it home in pieces, puzzled, never finding our place.

Mashing a life together and donning a smile.

Blanch

Fallen heroes have laid the foundation of my life.

Many survivors look back and wish they had the opportunity I have,

Alive, optimistic, with the hope of truly being,

Both feet settling in the sand,

Warm Atlantic tides wash over my toes,

Six feet deep and beyond.

People in pieces,

Enemies of the mirror,

Reflect their pains,

Deflect their fears,

Pray for relief,

Beg their handlers.

Glistening waves rise to my knees,

Standing tall on their knees,

Sand swirls in the retreating surf

As tornadic memories in their minds.

Surfers fall, their best effort to ride out the wave run aground

Six feet deep,

Yet there is a tether,

For their confident hero, bored, waits for them at the surface.

The Child That Would Be Missed

I missed the sunrise today.

I hope I live to see it return tomorrow,

For waves will run over the sand,

And the sun will set on my life.

Sit

Good boy, devil pup,

Fill the urine cup.

Still have a pulse?

Aw well,

We'll do what we must.

You're our headache to bear.

Here is a pill.

Now go and take care!

Wonderful Lights

Wonderful lights,

Gliding across the star-speckled sky,

Shining bright satellites,

Slicing through the fog of war.

Wonderful lights,

Candles blown out as Arab children wake to the chimes of ricochets.

Crimson tobacco illuminates my stoic face.

Smoke rises momentarily blotting out those distant infernos.

Wonderful lights,

Detonations recast a Humvee into a cremation chamber.

Gunship rockets flambé human flesh.

Wonderful lights go dark.

Minds twisted as mangled steel trucks,

Mines waiting to steal legs some bright mundane day.

There is a light at the end of this barrel.

Is it a wonderful light?

Let's look and see.

Cherish

Fear does not rise as this bullet kisses between my eyes,

Nor does anxiety as rockets shriek over my head.

Gangsters, crooked cops, and my enemies are lame,

So why do I have this fear I cannot tame?

Chaos and the fray from a once-peaceful day

Are more soothing than serene sunsets by the bay.

Dreams of awakening to a calm and fruitful life

Sting like pin pricks from the tip of a knife.

I'd live in my car, but I've the courage to try

To live some of that good life before I die,

Connecting with friends and hearts that care,

Relishing my hot dog instead of leaving it bare.

To taste and see the sun rise over the sea

As rays glide softly and brighten my smile,

It's time to enjoy the good life for a while.

The Bear and I

No words sung yet such great aching.

Why does this humming make my brain swell?

4 am, I sit in anguish,

Listening to my child cheerfully hum

As they piece together a puzzle in the candlelight.

I've eaten a hearty soup,

Savored my Colombian coffee,

Yet I remain agitated.

Around five hours of rest,

My ex-wife sleeps upstairs.

I am here.

My offspring reminds me of innocence,

The okay and healthy person that I am not.

I'll drink as soon as they leave.

Has numbing myself ever really helped?

Pain is there to tell me that there is an injury.

It's a signal that when struck,

Taking action to survive is needed.

Only by picking up the pieces

Will my shattered self become recognizable.

Broken shards of mirror across the bathroom floor and sink—

Like the stars before dawn, they glimmer with light as my many faces stare back.

Fragments of my soul have become star dust.

Small feet now rest in the bed.

The puzzle is finished

Save one missing piece from the skull of a panda.

He holds a sign that says, "Beach"

Just like me, the ocean drowns his worries. We may never find that piece,

Yet we can still hold on to those moments that make us feel whole.

Kabul Sunset

August 18, 2021,

15,000 Americans,

Millions of Afghans more,

Surrounded by the Taliban,

Ending NATO's longest war.

Women are bleeding in the streets.

Men are falling from the sky.

Babies are tossed over fences.

Mother's desperate hopes for a freer life.

Afghan leaders ran out the door,

Leaving all of them behind.

Brave Afghan soldiers are slaughtered in their homes

By a new moderate government so holy of mind.

American veterans lose brothers in arms

Far from the Carolina shore.

Afghan allies who bled and fought,

Those Taliban knocking at their door.

CHAPTER 3

Rest and Relaxation

Our Poem

Which are good poems, and which are not?

Which are hot, and which are cold?

Which are quiet and tame?

Which are defiant and bold?

Which tell of witches with stitches from conjuring rats?

Those of rats sucking blood, flying away as bats?

Mysteries, histories, or fantasy wombs,

Cleaning up the truth with infallible brooms?

If you know one poem, you may know them all.

These rhyme, those don't.

Some climb to a precipice with mighty long words.

Others are covered in droppings beneath lingering birds.

Whichever you read, try to be nice.

Poems are just words in a paragraphical orgy.

Some have Ss, some Ts, some Ds.

Many take vowels before they taste and C.

All are a mess, and all are the stars.

Many are there to be seen, a few to be ours.

Poetry bark can be rough or smooth.

Poetry's bark can bite or soothe.

We can't write better without being the writer who wrote,

For four is a number until it is opposite of aft.

Don't forget the four o'clock position is pretty far back.

I just realized I stopped rhyming; I must be out of whack!

It's just poetry yaw, spinning round.

Which poems are for you? How about this one you found?

Life and Liberty

Send these, the homeless tempest-tossed, to me.

Let them find a piece to lay their head at ease.

Our words converge. I find the urge to seize,

Grasp the day, come what may, I shall not sway,

Nor fret, regret, wish we never met, as horrors cause dismay,

For tomorrow's today

Is brighter than the stars,

When we know the day is ours.

Even behind the bars, freedom's fire chars.

Hardening my spear, I have no fear.

My mind is sharp. words flow like a harp,

Playing freedom reign, raining arrows from the sky like sparrows

For a peace to lay my head.

Personal Ad

Indomitable man

Annoyed easily,

Pleased sleazily,

The king of corny,

Emotionally thorny.

Lost my patients and my job,

Love to cook, am not a slob.

Seeks

Female of the age of consent,

Who doesn't smoke and has a sweet scent,

Old enough not to judge,

Who won't hold a grudge,

Satisfied with herself,

Joyous regardless of wealth.

My number is as disconnected as I am from the world.

I don't check my email

Or have my face in a book.

Reaching me is really quite hard,

But thanks for taking a look.

Kitchen Chorus

Shouts go off while working, jerking the chicken with allspice and curry,

Jokes abound, clashing shades of skin,

Cheesy smiles, and wheels of gouda,

Round-bellied cooks grinning like Buddha,

Singing Syrah, Syrah,[1] what never can be can't be,

Wine flowing like crisp winter streams,

Thoughts are tortellini floating in serene soup bowls in our dreams.

As tastebuds swim in bliss,

Our lips collide like this (*kiss*).

No worries for us in this time.

Sweet peace fills our mouths and minds,

Mends our pains, and sews our rhymes.

The world can just spin away

If you'll only hold my hand.

---

[1] Full-bodied wine with subtle fresh black fruit notes and black pepper.

Eric Sowers

Comings and Goings

Pixie's flutter from my dreams,

Sprinkling fairy dust over sweet candy streams.

Parched from sugar, carrot in hand,

I'm a wabbit. I'm a bunny, healthy and bland.

'Tis this hare unseasoned? Is there no flavor to be had?

Is this hopping and never stopping furry creature just a fad?

I taste like—who knows? Eat me and see.

You'll find I'm a lyrical delicacy.

Have some words for your mind.

I like to wave my dictionary around.

Vocabulary is so tasty. look here, the word ground!

Ground beef with some cheese for carnivores in a car.

Veggie bowls and salad you can find at a bar.

Bars have exquisite beer, so don't get barred from your pub.

Get a law degree, join the Bar and plead your case.

Raise the bar in your field as you win your race.

Have a beer with some nuts. Have a seat in the back.

View the comings and goings, coming here, going there.

View the no-shows and showings.

View the garbed and the bare.

The Child That Would Be Missed

Don't leave your glass for Mickey to sip.

Let fools boast until exhausted. Just relax don't take a trip.

It's a wonderful life we have when we make wise choices,

When we ignore foolish words, and heed mindful voices.

Through the Ups and Downs

Today,

The sun is coming up,

Then going down,

And though your face may frown,

Remember to raise a smile in the morning,

When the sun comes back around.

CHAPTER 4

Sight Alignment and Sight Picture

Global Climate Crisis

We've become polarized bears,

And the temperature is rising,

Our patience is melting,

Our virtual habitat, congested,

Our appetite for each other's folly.

We're flooded with conflicts before our opinions take shape,

So we abort them and adopt those of our tribe.

We become I, and our eyes are bloodshot from the screens.

I Am the American Flag

I can't only be white

Unless you surrender,

So don't be blue.

I'm still waving true.

Don't tread on me,

You who are filled with hate.

Even I take a knee to grieve.

I kneel for our heroes

Whether dark or light.

I burn bright for your freedom,

As you fight for your rights.

Love me or hate me,

I'm still exclaiming a just dream for you,

Where your blood isn't ransom,

For a little security

Where paltry mistakes aren't an end to your life and liberty.

Unfurling a greater nation takes most of you

Loving today

Without forgetting yesterday.

May each star honor you.

The Child That Would Be Missed

Don't let me be hung on the rope.

Let me fly free in the sunlight.

When I am stained and torn,

Don't toss me to the street and drive over me.

I was born from Britain's oppression.

Africans bore America's Constitutional concession.

By their stripes we revealed

It takes not all but most of you.

Feel the thundering voice inside.

Shout out! Don't let fear purvey silence.

Don't dawn a special flag just for you.

It takes most of you

To make freedom ring for all of you.

Knowing Your Right......From Left

They just told me I'm wrong.

Thankfully, I know that I'm right,

For my right is their wrong,

And their right is my plight,

Yet neither of us are in error

For how we perceive or feel.

Rightfully right, knowing their right is not left,

Yet it is left to me to decide how it should be for me.

No need to speedily say

That I am incorrect today.

Your words stumble from your lips,

Drunken from delusion and fantasy.

No thanks, none for me.

Instead, I'll raise the anchor,

And search for a mind anchored in reality.

For the horizon is clear of clouds— how can you not see?

Even the squawking fowl of the air agree with me!

If only I were you, you could be right too!

What's that you utter?

Dock my words. release the rudder?

The Child That Would Be Missed

While the wind fills your sails

And the truth prevails?

Now in your sea, I cannot see

Or pierce this fog surrounding me.

This hand I feel cannot be real,

For there is nothing in front of my eyes.

A hand touches my face,

Fingers I can barely see.

But not my hand, so which one could it be?

We've finally connected.

You've got it right on the nose.

We were wrong to be right for each other,

Yet right to be wrung of this mental clutter.

We may not see eye to eye

Nor embrace each other's truth.

Truth be told, my truths not that old.

Yes, I once agreed with you.

Wait, here we are just two.

Is there another point of view?

No Quarter

As decades advance

And we wake from our trance,

We will realize about us versus them.

No matter the skin we wear

Or the faith we lay bare,

There truly is no them there.

It's always been us from birth

Since we first set foot on this earth,

From that first small step for man

To giant leaps for womankind,

And when we join hands to lift up those we left behind,

It is still us, no matter how hard we try.

Pointing missiles and fingers

To then and now,

To you and I,

To why and how.

Differences won't justify indifference.

Distances won't depreciate our worth.

For we are one until the last day is done

And one last step touches this earth.

Melancholy

I long for a time when the world left its bullshit at the door.

None wandered in.

No paper in hand.

Just quiet and silence to comprehend.

Disease may get you and your kids.

Mason jars may preserve you with those boiled-tight lids.

No lights to keep my eyes toiling.

Just the dancing candle revealing my words,

Black and silent as the darkness.

Silent Bee

I looked down onto the floor of my SUV.

There lay a honey bee looking up at me.

Her abdomen throbbing, she licked her leg,

Alone, unafraid, foreseeing her end.

Struggling to rise, standing, wings spread,

Then collapsing to the floor but not quite dead.

I considered ending it, taking her out of this pain,

Yet in this natural end to a life on the fly,

I decided to share these moments with her.

Licking her leg again, they began to flail outstretched.

For moments she shook as she cringed back to her feet,

Falling one last time, outstretching her body,

Then curling up into the fetal position.

Looking up into my eyes, she remained motionless,

Only a shell remained of a bee-u-tiful life.

Sky of Wonder

Across a pink accented sky,

Where the sun stood not long before,

Lay drops of love in the clouds above,

Ready to descend in a downpour.

Those golden clouds reflect the day's last rays,

Holding in their feelings,

Not letting them out,

And all I can do is gaze.

What wonderful love is up in that sky

Hidden behind now moonlit puffs,

Slowly drifting toward the horizon,

While the chill of night begins to nibble on my earlobe.

I'm apprehensive that love won't reign today.

Slight dread fills my drooping head

As drops find their way to the ground.

I turn every which way. No other drops can be found.

Wiping my face, I gaze up again

At a clear and crisp starry night.

Wish Me Well

Pennies I barely knew

Sunk to the bottom of the fountain,

For I was told, with little effort,

I could reach the top of that mountain.

Then, I dug a hole deeper than that coin.

Along the path to begin the climb, wishy flowers with all their seeds,

"Pick one, blow it into the wind, and your wish will come true,"

Yet no wish was granted as those baby flowers flew.

Work a secure job, and save for retirement

Is a seed that drifts until your life is spent,

Until you sink to the bottom,

And no wishes come true.

So I stopped wishing, and now I am sailing out of view.

Can't Be

When they say that nothing can be done,

There's something we can do.

We can choose to be the crazy one,

Who makes what can't come true.

When our mind is strapped to find

Some milk to find the whey,

Remember, it's in there, so bring it out,

And you'll gain curds along the way.

How many times it couldn't happen,

And how many moments we decided it would,

Our eyes wide with pride,

When from nothing came something good.

Eric Sowers

This Is It!

Here it is folks,

The words that you've been waiting for,

The ones that will change your life,

Not just make you drop the knife,

Preserve you through strife,

Almighty and grand a lyrical keg stand,

Topping you off with courage,

Syphoning bad vibes,

Silencing rotten jibes,

One world just the way it should be,

Serene, safe, warm, happy.

Are you ready for the cure

To life's misery?

To broken hearts, wretched farts, and poverty?

Here it is, all you need to know—

What Are You Looking At?

Agony and anxiety,

Loathing these thoughts, fearing no change will be.

I don't want to rhyme. Just forget about me.

Let me fade into darkness,

Quiet and calm,

No rebounding, no resounding, "Yes! I love life!"

I pity the fool in the mirror.

He doesn't have to see this glum fantasy.

His eyes see himself so much clearer!

Such a loving soul, only a slight jerk,

No one is perfect, just needs a little work.

A man with much pain, who is kind to strangers,

Funny in lots of meanings of the word,

Puts a smile on my face every time!

He grows on you like moss on a sloth.

He will always have your back when jaguars creep near.

Just do your poop dance and have no fear.

Maybe you're like him, and those sweet eyes in the mirror

See the real you, see your beauty much clearer.

Will change be for you and I?

We will never be free unless we try.

How Do I Reel In That Fish?

Reel in the wish from that star?

Reeling in agony from broken dreams,

Shards sunken in murky streams,

I have half a mind, too.

Go and do something sane.

Live days in the sun, exchanging words,

Truly trading moments while singing gibberish.

Want, wanton, what do I need?

Have you met my needs? They're ridiculous.

The wants are worse, changing day to day.

Pitter patter, the mini schnauzer skims across the laminate floor.

If only it were hardwood from some extinct tree, alas.

This wood is no good.

A façade like my chest, covering the cold cement heart beneath.

Will I be remembered? No.

Maybe for a time.

Hopefully, not a crime.

May I be recalled smiling.

You Can't Fix Stupid

I'm glad I can't fix stupid,

For I would feel obligated every day

Just like Cupid with his arrows

To fling intelligence every which way.

Through the window of the slow driver,

Crawling in the leftmost lane.

In the eye of my nosy neighbor.

And in the hateful's flaming urethra.

I'd fly around fixing dumb until my time runs out

Just to find that I missed the mark,

Forgetting

What life is truly about.

Heel of Achilles

We are our breath until death,

Our lifetime the breeze dancing with the leaves.

As the jet stream, I am unable to slow.

Earth and my head spin in a constant flow.

To be in my life, you must hold on tight.

Come see the world. Though it is clear to see,

I want to hide the pain within me.

For this tempest hails from solemn blue skies

And quickly leaves a mess, scarring both our lives.

Bringing us back—to what happened here?

Then leaves settle, resting on the grass,

And silence wins the day.

Our breath becomes still

In the eye of the storm.

Close Enough

Beauty is in the eyes of the beholder,

Yet I cannot see her beauty or hold her

2,

5,

Or 1,000,000 hectares away.

These eyes are for her in every way,

Not simply the effervescent smile on her face

Or the warmth when our palms embrace.

On the worst day her smile sets misery to flight.

Though I can't see her, she's everything in sight.

A Drop of Water

Good morrow my day.

Plopping drops splash hither and nye.

I'm ready, fully prepared for what comes my way.

Dance and wave hello to the gray bearded sky.

I've drawn water from a new well,

One that is pure and clear.

How those drops will run through me, I cannot tell—

Either sweat, blood, or tear.

Sweating in the forge of my passions,

Bleeding my words onto this page,

Tear after tear for a world void of compassion,

Or none of these in my rage.

Does my passion make the world more compassionate?

Do my words bleed into your soul?

Will my tears dispel my rage?

I plead for yes.

Without Compare

Like these poems I've written,

The meow of a kitten,

There are things that must not go unsaid.

Just as books should not be burned

Nor warriors left for dead.

Not as lovers love,

Nor for the love for a mother,

Nor just a friend,

I love you.

In no way I can describe,

A writer without words,

An unfathomable kind of love.

CREDITS

Beta Readers

Abantika Bose (@hjbookblog)

Jacob Kydan

Klaudia Kicsak

Rita Liu

Taiba Tabassum

Book Cover

Stephen Rocktaschel

Editor

Eric Muhr

Public Relations

Jennifer Le

THE AUTHOR

After over a decade in the Marine Corps, Eric and his family moved back into their home in rural North Carolina. Though he would not return to Iraq or Afghanistan, his memories brought the war back to him as he struggled to be a father and husband. Through the flames of rage, shame, and addiction, Eric persevered to discover moments of joy and a path to inner peace.

www.ingramcontent.com/pod-product-compliance
Lightning Source LLC
Chambersburg PA
CBHW030540180626
46810CB00005B/1956